Spiders Everywhere!

Contents	**Page**
Are spiders insects?	2-3
Habitat	4-5
Pest control	6-7
Webs	8-9
Silk	10-11
Diet	12-13
Body parts	14-15
Enemies	16-17
Spiderlings	18-19
Moving	20-21
Species	22-23
Index	24

written by Rachel Walker

Are spiders insects?

No, spiders are not insects, and they are different to insects in lots of ways. Spiders belong to a group called arachnids, which have two body parts: the front body section, and an abdomen. Insects have three body parts: a head, thorax, and abdomen. Spiders have eight legs, but insects have only six legs. Most spiders have "simple" eyes instead of "compound" eyes that give lots of insects better eyesight.

insects

spider eyes

3

Where do spiders live?

Spiders live in your house, in your classroom, in the garden, in every country in the world. They live on every continent except Antarctica. There are over 40,000 different species! Some float **on** the water, such as fishing spiders, and some even live **under** the water, such as diving bell spiders.

Australia's wolf spider

Australia is home to a number of spider species and has the highest number of poisonous spiders in any country. The most dangerous ones include the funnel web spider and its family: the red back, the wolf spider, the white tail, and the mouse spider. The funnel web spider is believed to be the most venomous species in the world.

What use are spiders?

Spiders are extremely important to farming and horticulture. They are predators, and their main prey is insects, many of which eat our crops and pester our livestock. As natural pest controllers they are particularly useful.

wheat

Spiders are also food for many animals, and even humans – tarantulas are considered a delicious treat in many countries! Medical researchers are studying the chemicals in spider venom for use in treating diseases in people.

What about webs?

Spiders are famous for the intricate webs they weave out of strong strands of protein called silk. All spiders can make silk in their bodies and push it out between special body parts called spinnerets at the end of the spider's abdomen. New webs can be built every single day. Sticky webs are a great way to catch a meal! Lessons learned from spider web structures are helping engineers who design bridges.

spiders help engineers

Spider silk

People have been making use of spider silk for thousands of years. It is incredibly strong, light, and useful, as it's the strongest known natural material – in equal weight it is even stronger than steel! The Australian Aborigines used silk as fishing lines for small fish, and the ancient Greeks used cobwebs to stop wounds from bleeding. More recently, spider silk was used as the crosshairs in guns and telescopes, and people of the Solomon Islands still use it as fishing nets.

What do they eat?

Most species trap small insects and other spiders in their webs for food. A few large species of spiders prey on small birds, snakes and lizards. One species is vegetarian, feeding on acacia trees. Some baby spiders eat plant nectar. In captivity, spiders have been known to eat egg yolk, bananas, marmalade, milk and sausages. Spiders eat a lot for their size, and can eat their own weight in one meal! They can then go without food for a long time.

Parts of a spider

Spiders need all eight of their legs to run, climb and jump. Luckily, if a leg is lost the injured spider can gradually grow a replacement. Spiders have at least two claws on the end of each leg to help them climb smooth surfaces like glass. Some have six eyes and some have eight. There are smooth-skinned types and hairy ones. Some are tiny, but others, like the tarantula, are the size of your hand.

Enemies

Birds and wasps are the main enemies of spiders, but they can also be prey to other insects, lizards, bats, fish, frogs and toads. Some species are even cannibals that eat other spiders! Most species need camouflage to avoid these enemies, so many types are black or brown with patterns to blend with trees and earth. But there are also some bright spiders: red, yellow, green, white, blue and orange, as well as spotted or striped.

Eggs

18

Many female spiders lay hundreds of eggs into an egg sac that is carried under the body, or hidden under a rock or piece of bark. They guard the eggs for three weeks until they hatch into tiny spiderlings. The mother continues to stay close for several more weeks as they develop.

Can spiders fly?

No, spiders can't fly, but some spiderlings "balloon." When a young spider balloons, it points its abdomen in the air and sends out a long thread of very fine silk, called gossamer. Wind catches the light thread and carries the spider away. Spiderlings have been known to travel long distances doing this, although most don't go far.

Names

Among the thousands of spider species, there are some very unusual names:

- huntsman
- black widow
- cannibal
- crab-leg
- trapdoor
- money spider
- sun spider
- jumping spider
- wolf spider

What can you add to this list?

black widow

Index

	Page
body parts	2, 14
camouflage	16
eggs	18-19
habitat	4-5
poison	5, 7
predators	6, 16
prey	6, 12-13
silk	8, 10
species	4-5, 12, 16, 23
spiderlings	19, 20
usefulness	6-7, 8, 10
webs	8, 12